The Birthday Party

PUFFIN PIED PIPER BOOKS
Published by the Penguin Group
Penguin Books USA Inc., 375 Hudson Street, New York, New York 10014, U.S.A.
Penguin Books Ltd, 27 Wrights Lane, London W8 5TZ, England
Penguin Books Australia Ltd, Ringwood, Victoria, Australia
Penguin Books Canada Ltd, 10 Alcorn Avenue, Toronto, Ontario, Canada M4V 3B2
Penguin Books (N.Z.) Ltd, 182-190 Wairau Road, Auckland 10, New Zealand
Penguin Books Ltd, Registered Offices: Harmondsworth, Middlesex, England

First published in the United States 1983
by Dial Books for Young Readers
A Division of Penguin Books USA Inc.

Published in Great Britain by Walker Books, Inc.
Copyright © 1983 by Helen Oxenbury
All rights reserved
Library of Congress Catalog Card Number: 82-19792
Printed in Hong Kong
First Puffin Pied Piper Printing 1993
ISBN 0-14-054947-1
1 3 5 7 9 10 8 6 4 2
A Pied Piper Book is a registered trademark of
Dial Books for Young Readers, a division of Penguin Books USA Inc.,
® TM 1,163,686 and ® TM 1,054,312.

The Birthday Party

by Helen Oxenbury

A Puffin Pied Piper

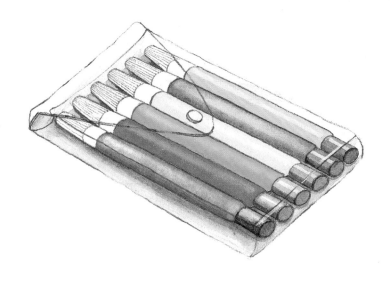

I chose John's birthday
present all by myself.

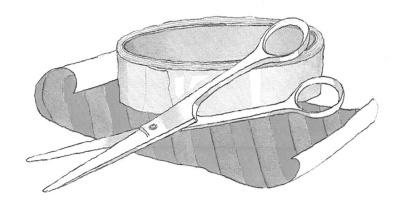

"Can't I try them, Mommy?"
"No," Mommy said, "we bought
them for John."

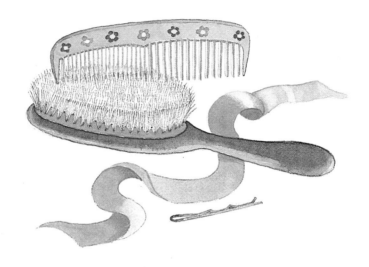

"I'll fix your hair and then we can leave for the party," said Mommy.

"What did you bring me?" John
asked when we arrived.

"Happy birthday, John,"
Mommy said.
She made me give him the present.

"Here's my cake," John shouted.
He left my present just lying
on the floor.

After we ate, we played games
and made a big mess.

My daddy came to pick me up.
"Give her the balloon,"
John's mother said.
"Do you really want it?"
asked John.
"Do I ever!" I said.

About the Author/Artist

Helen Oxenbury is internationally recognized as one of the finest children's book illustrators, with over thirty books to her credit, including *We're Going on a Bear Hunt* and *The Dragon of an Ordinary Family* (Dial) by Margaret Mahy. Her Very First Books®—five board books for toddlers—have been newly designed and reissued by Dial. According to *The Washington Post,* the books "will delight parents and entertain infants." *The Bulletin of the Center for Children's Books* applauded, "Fun, but more than that: These are geared to the toddler's interests and experiences." Ms. Oxenbury lives in London.